KT-433-293

For Kit with love – then, now and always
~ AD

For Otilie and George, the other little monkeys!
~ KMcE

SIMON AND SCHUSTER
First published in Great Britain in 2006 by Simon and Schuster UK Ltd
Africa House, 64-78 Kingsway, London WC2B 6AH

This paperback edition first published in 2007

Book designed by Genevieve Webster
The text for this book is set in Cochin
The illustrations for this book are rendered in watercolour and coloured pencil

A CIP catalogue record for this book is available from the British Library upon request

ISBN10: 0689 87482 0
ISBN13: 9780689874826

Printed in China
1 3 5 7 9 8 6 4 2

I LOVE YOU, LITTLE MONKEY

Alan Durant &
Katharine McEwen

SIMON AND SCHUSTER
London New York Sydney

Little Monkey was bored.
Big Monkey was picking figs
for supper, so Little Monkey
had no one to play with.
"Why don't you do some
climbing?" said Big Monkey.
"You like climbing."

Little Monkey climbed up
to the top of the Big Tree
and he climbed down again.

He saw a pile of figs on the
ground. He picked one up.
It was ripe and squashy.

He threw it at the trunk
of the Big Tree.

Splat!

Little Monkey laughed.

He threw another fig. . .
and another.

When Big Monkey came back there were no figs left, just a squishy mess. "That was naughty, Little Monkey," he said. "Those figs were for our supper! Now I'll have to go and pick some more."

"I'll help you," said Little Monkey.
So Little Monkey helped Big Monkey
pick figs for supper.
"Now will you play with me?"
asked Little Monkey.

"Not yet," said Big Monkey.
"First, I've got to make the beds.
Why don't you do some swinging
and jumping? You like swinging
and jumping."

Little Monkey swung and
jumped on the Big Tree.

Then he saw the bed that
Big Monkey had made for him.
It looked lovely and soft and
springy. It looked just right
for jumping on.

Wheee!

Little Monkey jumped.

Whumpf!

He landed right in the middle
of the bed and crushed it.
Big Monkey shook his head
and frowned.
"Oh, that was naughty,
Little Monkey," he said.
"Now I'll have to make your
bed all over again."

"I'll help you,"
said Little Monkey.

Little Monkey helped
Big Monkey make his bed again.
"*Now* will you play with me?"
Little Monkey asked.

Big Monkey yawned.
"First I need a little nap,"
he said. "All that extra work
has made me tired.
Why don't you play up in
the Big Tree for a while?"
Big Monkey lay down
on his bed.

Little Monkey played on his own.

He ran and sprang
and jumped. He lay on
his back and wiggled
his legs in the air.

Then he played a game
of falling and catching
in the Big Tree.

He fell off one
branch and caught
hold of another.

Down and down
he dropped, until he
was just above
where Big Monkey
was sleeping.
Then . . .

Whoops!

He landed right on top
of Big Monkey!

Big Monkey was very cross.

"You naughty little monkey!" he shouted.

"Go up to your bed now!"

Little Monkey climbed
up to his bed.

He started to cry.

Big Monkey went up to Little Monkey.

"You don't love me," Little Monkey sobbed.

"I do, Little Monkey," said Big Monkey.

"You know I do."

"You don't love me when
I'm naughty," said Little Monkey.

"Yes I do," said Big Monkey. "I may not like
the naughty things you do sometimes,
but I love you always, even when you're naughty."

Little Monkey still looked sad.
"I know, let's play swing-and-chase," said Big Monkey.
Little Monkey smiled. Swing-and-chase
was his favourite game.

They played and played . . . until at last
they came to a clearing around a large pool.
They stopped and had a drink.

"That was fun!" said Little Monkey.
"Yes, it was," said Big Monkey.

Big Monkey took Little Monkey's
paw in his own.

"I'm sorry I did those naughty things,
Big Monkey," said Little Monkey.

Big Monkey smiled.
"I'm sorry I shouted at you," he said.
"Yes," said Little Monkey,
"it was naughty to shout at me."

Big Monkey gave Little Monkey
a great big hug.

"I love you, Little Monkey," he said.

"Climb onto my back," said Big Monkey,
"and I'll carry you home."

Little Monkey climbed onto Big Monkey's back.
He put his arms around Big Monkey's neck.

"I love you too, Big Monkey,"

he whispered.

"I love you . . . even when you're naughty."